REGULAR SHOW
Fakespeare in the Park

BY GABE SORIA

CARTOON NETWORK BOOKS
An Imprint of Penguin Random House

CARTOON NETWORK BOOKS
Penguin Young Readers Group
An Imprint of Penguin Random House LLC

Photo credit: pages 106–133: (parchment paper) © Thinkstock/iStock/fotoluk1983

ISBN 978-0-8431-8345-0 10 9 8 7 6 5 4 3 2 1

DRAMATIS PERSONAE

(In Order of Appearance)

Cronella, a Witch

Blandene, another Witch

Putricia, the third Witch

Benson, a Boss

Mordecai, a Fool

Rigby, another Fool

The Gods of Theater

Pops, a Gentle Soul

Muscle Man, a Lout

Hi-Five Ghost, a Ghost

Skips, a Sage

Thomas, an Apprentice

Gene, a rival Boss

The Merrie Players, a Band of Traveling Actors

C.J., a Maiden

Eileen, her Second

Galahad Thrillington, the leader of the Merrie Players

Death, the personification of Mortality

William Shakespeare, a Spirit

Larry the Laser Wizard, a Keyboardist

— PROLOGUE —

GONGGGGGGG . . . GONGGGGGGG . . . GONGGGGGGG. The bell in the clock tower in the town square began to ring twelve long and spooky times. On the craggy hilltop overlooking the sleeping city, three figures gathered 'round a cauldron bubbling over a fire, going about their weird business. It was midnight—the witching hour. And in this case, we mean *witching hour* literally, because the three figures were honest-to-goodness WITCHES, and midnight is their time to shine.

"The chimes have sounded, my sisters!" said Cronella, the eldest of the three. She looked the most like a traditional "witchy" witch—she was dressed in pointy shoes, striped socks, gray rags, and a pointed hat. She jabbed a bony finger in the direction of the town's glittering lights. "Look yonder! There it is, the humble place where soon a great reckoning shall occur!"

Her sister Blandene looked up from the cauldron, into which she was sprinkling some salt from the shaker she had just taken out of her fanny pack. Blandene was dressed a tad less traditionally than Cronella; she liked to wear jeans and an oversize sweater with a kitty cat on it. She squinted in the general direction her sister's gnarly finger was aiming.

"There's going to be a great reckoning at the bowling alley?" said Blandene. "Great! Do we get to go? I haven't been bowling in, like, forever."

"No, not the bowling alley! Cast your eyes widdershins," said Cronella.

"Widder-what?" said the third sister, Putricia, who didn't look up at all. Putricia, being the youngest sister, was dressed like a mall goth. She was sitting cross-legged on the ground, focused on the handheld video game she was playing.* "And is that stew ready yet? I'm starrrrrrving."

"What kind of witches are you that you don't even know what *widdershins* means? I mean, c'mon! Was I the only one paying attention in class? I . . ." Cronella sighed and took a deep breath. *In through the nose, out through the mouth.* Her doctor had warned her about her blood pressure. "The left. A little over to the left of the bowling alley."

"Oh, okay. The LEFT." Blandene squinted harder as she looked to the left of the bowling alley. "At Taco'Clock? Even better. They have the BEST guacamole, and their chips are homemade."

Putricia looked up from her game. "Did I hear someone say *Taco'Clock*? Omigod, let's go. Their guacamole is the BOMB."

"No, your OTHER left, you idiots."

"Rats. I was really looking forward to that guacamole," said Blandene. She and Putricia joined

---

**Witch Wars*, a totally awesome side-scrolling and top-down shooting game where you play as a witch flying on a broom who has to blast her way through multiple levels of insanity in Supernatural Space.

Cronella at the edge of the cliff to get a better look. "Okay, to the left . . . Hmm. Oh! You mean the Park?"

"Yes! The Park."

"Why didn't you just say that in the first place?" said Putricia.

"Because it's cooler and more mysterious to just point and say, 'Look yonder,' that's why!" Cronella threw her hands up. "We're weird! We're witches! Being mysterious is our thing. Duh!"

"Well, you don't have to get so bent out of shape about it," Putricia said, with a roll of her eyes.

"I'm NOT bent out of shape! I just take this weird-sisters thing seriously, okay?"

"Okay, you two. Break it up." Being the middle sister, Blandene was used to having to come between the other two witches. "So, what's the plan?"

"The plan is this: We shall go to the Park, set up shop there, and watch these amazing events unfold," said Cronella. "When necessary, we'll give advice to the players in this drama. You know, standard witch stuff."

"Sounds good," said Blandene. "Do you have some sort of scary prophecy to say before we eat and hit the road?"

"I thought you'd never ask!" Cronella waved her hands around in a witchy manner, and the fire below the cauldron flared up, lighting her face dramatically from below. In the distance, lightning began to crackle, and thunder boomed, even though the night was cloudless. Cronella began to speak:

A globe-headed King,
His brow bedecked with worry,
Annoyed by two Knaves
Who hath inspired his fury.
The Players shall fall,
A Spirit will rise,
To say any more
T'would spoil the surprise.

A spooky silence fell over the witches' circle, a silence soon pierced by the appreciative slow clapping of Blandene and Putricia.

"That was very nice, Cronella," said Blandene. "Excellent job!"

"Yes! Real awesome prophesying. I got goose bumps," said Putricia, who held out her arm for her sister to inspect. She did, indeed, have goose bumps.

Cronella closed her eyes and put a hand to her heart. "Thanks, sisters. That means a lot to me. Even now, the King sleeps, perchance to dream of the events to come. We shall see him and his anonymous crew. But for now: It's chowtime!"

The witches ladled witch stew into their bowls and began to eat, and here we shall leave them, for they have terrible table manners and they're kind of gross to watch. Thus our prologue ends, and using the magic of literature (and theater), we switch our scene as our story REALLY begins . . .

CHAPTER 1

"Aaaaaaaaaah! Nooooooooo!"

Benson screamed as he jumped out of bed still half asleep, trying to put out an invisible fire. His tangled sheets twisted around his legs, and he fell to the floor with a thump. Panting, he looked around. He wasn't back there, back then. It was now, and he was in his bedroom, in his apartment. And he was okay. Kind of.

"The same dream again," he muttered. "Every night for the past week, I've dreamt that I'm back there reliving that terrible night when . . . no—that's all in the past. There's nothing I can do to change it. I have to look to the future."

Getting up, he stumbled into his kitchen, where his automatic coffeemaker was already making a fresh pot of java. He squinted in the glare of the bright red light from the coffeemaker's clock: six o'clock in the morning, almost time to go to work. Taking his favorite mug from the cupboard, Benson poured himself a cup of coffee and went to the kitchen window. The sun was just beginning to rise, and it bathed him in the glorious golden light of dawn, making him look super impressive.

"It's time to do some really positive thinking. If everything goes according to plan, today the Park turns a page, and a new era begins," Benson said with a smile. He took a satisfied sip and smiled again. *This is a really good cup of coffee.*

"Everything is going to be just GREAT . . . as long as those boneheads Mordecai and Rigby don't screw it up." Benson closed his eyes and crossed his fingers. "Please don't let them screw it up, Theater Gods. Pleasepleaseplease."

And that, dear reader, is what we call

FORESHADOWING. Pay attention, because something crazy is going to happen, and it's going to happen VERY soon.

⟡

A few hours and many cups of coffee later, Benson stood in front of the house in the Park that served as Park headquarters. In one hand he held a clipboard, and under his arm was a roll of papers. Pops, Muscle Man, Hi-Five Ghost, Skips, and Thomas all sat on the house's front steps, talking among themselves. Mordecai and Rigby were punching each other on the shoulder, trying to give the other one a dead arm. Benson cleared his throat for silence, and after a few moments, everybody quieted down.

"All right, everybody. Listen up," Benson said. "As you know, in a few days we're having the Park's annual Shakespeare Festival, and every year we compete against Gene and the guys over at East Pines to put on the best summer Shakespeare Festival in town. You probably also know that every year they win the audience poll and take home the Gilded Globe."

"Last year their version of *Doctor Faustus* blew that puppet show you hired off the stage. Literally!" said Skips. "That pyro was somethin' else."

"They're unbeatable, Benson. Give it up already," said Mordecai.

"Yeah," said Rigby. "This year let's just put in the least amount of effort on another lame puppet show and move on to cooler things."

Benson put up his hands for silence.

"Well, this year's going to be different, I promise you. I've got a surprise in store for East Pines AND the town. I've been saving discretionary money for years to be able to afford this, but this year our headlining act is going to be—get this—the MERRIE PLAYERS."

Benson unrolled one of the papers under his

arm with a flourish, revealing a poster decorated at the top with a drawing of the masks of comedy and tragedy, under which it read, in fancy calligraphy, "Shakespeare Festival at the Park featuring the world-famous MERRIE PLAYERS performing a TOP-SECRET PLAY by the one and only SHAKESPEARE—It's the SHAKES-PERIENCE of the CENTURY!" The guys on the steps whistled and murmured among themselves, impressed.

"Hey, nonny-nonny!" said Muscle Man. "I LOVE the Merrie Players! They're, like, the Fist Pump of traveling Shakespeare companies. You know who else likes traveling Shakespearean theater companies?" Muscle Man took off his shirt and spun it over his head. "My mom! Woo-hoo!"

"Good show, Benson!" said Pops. "Or rather, it WILL be. Hee, hee, hee!"

"Thank you, Muscle Man and Pops. It's good to know that there are at least a couple of real theater fans around here. But even though I've got the unbeatable Merrie Players coming, there's still plenty of stuff to do in order to make the show perfect. So let's go down the list and see where we're at with our preparations. Skips: How's construction coming on the replica Elizabethan London theater I ordered from Stör? Is it authentic?"

Skips gave Benson a thumbs-up. "I've been building it over in the back meadow, and it's almost finished. You'll think you're back in 1602, believe me—I was there, and it's TOTALLY period correct, down to having no bathrooms. Those guys at Stör really know their stuff."

"Fantastic! Gross, but fantastic," said Benson as he made a check mark on his clipboard. "Pops, you're in charge of the concessions. Are we going to have enough turkey legs and soda for the crowds?"

"Oh, indeed, Benson. Turkey legs and root beer for all!"

Benson made another check on his list. "Excellent! If these posters work out, I'm expecting us to be at capacity. And speaking of crowds, Muscle Man and Hi-Five Ghost, you guys are on ticket duty and security."

Muscle Man stood up and made two fists. "You got it, Benson! We'll take the tickets, and if anybody tries to sneak in, we'll PUNCH their tickets, right, Fives?"

"You said it, Muscle Man," replied Hi-Five Ghost, who clenched his ghostly head hand in a fist, too.

"Great," said Benson, who then focused his attention on Thomas, the Park's former intern. "Thomas, your time as an intern has convinced me to give you one of the most important jobs this week: The Merrie Players are arriving today, and I want you to be their factotum."

"What?!" screamed Rigby, throwing up his hands. "How come Thomas gets to be the factotum? I wanna be the factotum. Being a factotum sounds cool.

By the way: What's a factotum?"

Benson sighed. "A factotum, Rigby, is someone who can be of assistance."

"I can totally do that! I'm, like, the most helpful guy around here."

After everyone had finished snickering, Benson said, "Usually a factotum is someone who can be of assistance competently and do things—sometimes HARD things—without complaining."

Rigby's eyes widened, and he turned to Thomas. "Ohhhhhh. I see. Good luck with being the factotum, Thomas."

Benson rolled his eyes and made another mark on his list, and Mordecai cleared his throat.

"Ahem! Uh, it sounds like you've got everything wrapped up, Benson," Mordecai said. "Maybe Rigby and I can, you know, just kinda supervise everybody and stuff." He smiled and laughed nervously.

"Oh no you don't. It's all hands on deck for the

festival. I've got a job for you guys that should be impossible to screw up."

"Never say impossible, Benson," said Rigby.

Benson twisted his mouth into a grimace and tossed the roll of posters under his arm to Mordecai.

"You two are the advertising crew. I need you guys to go into town and put these posters up everywhere you can. In coffee shops, on poles—anywhere there's some space, there should be a poster. We've gotta get the word out that this year's Shakespeare Festival at the Park is the one to see."

"Awww, but Benson—there's a marathon of Jake Rock films showing downtown this weekend at the Ritz: *Occult Cop*, *Real Bad Dudez*, *Occult Cops*, *Occult Cops Meet the Real Bad Dudez* . . ."

"I'm sorry, Rigby, but this is way more important than Jake Rock movies."

"What did you say?! More important than Jake Rock?!"

Mordecai grinned sheepishly at Benson and held up a finger. "Hold on a second."

Mordecai pulled Rigby down and whispered into his ear, "Dude, shut up. Think about it. We'll just walk around town with the posters and put a few up, then go to the arcade and visit C.J. and Eileen. It's practically like getting a free day off."

"You're right, Mordecai," whispered Rigby. "Awesome plan." Rigby quickly turned to Benson. "Okay, Benson. You've convinced us. We'll definitely be the advertising guys."

Benson rolled his eyes. "You do realize that I'm your *boss* and I don't have to *convince*. That you *have* to do what I say or else you're *fired*, right?"

Mordecai and Rigby grinned and gave Benson two thumbs-up.

"Fine, whatever. Just put the posters up."

Benson looked at the list on his clipboard and made a second-to-last check mark. *This IS going to work,* he thought. But there was one remaining item to address.

"This is great, guys. One last item on the agenda and then we can get to work: I've gotten some reports of three ladies dressed kind of like witches setting up tents in the Park at the old abandoned campground. Mordecai and Rigby, before you go out on poster duty, go over there and check it out. If you see these women, please politely but firmly inform them that the Park closes at eleven p.m. and that it is NOT an open-air hotel. Besides, that's where the Merrie Players are going to set up camp."

"Whoa, whoa, whoa—did you say 'witches'? That's above my pay grade," said Rigby.

"Yeah, man," said Mordecai. "Haven't you heard the saying? 'Witches give stitches.'"

"Witches give stitches!" Rigby echoed, and together he and Mordecai began to chant:

"Witches give stitches / And pains in yo' britches

/ When your eyelid twitches / It's probably 'cause of witches!"

"Shut up and just do it, okay?!" Benson yelled. He made a final check mark on his list. "And that's that. Okay, team—I'm counting on you guys to help make this the greatest Shakespeare Festival the town's EVER seen. In the immortal words of the Bard himself, 'Be not afraid of greatness: Some are born great, some achieve greatness, and some have greatness thrust upon 'em.'[1] Now let's get ready for greatness!"

Everybody nodded, impressed by Benson's words, and went off to go to work. Everybody except Mordecai and Rigby, who looked confused.

"Who's this Bard guy?" asked Rigby. "I thought we were talking about Shakespeare. Ow! Why'd you hit me?"

"The Bard IS Shakespeare, dude," said

---

[1] Spoken by Malvolio in Shakespeare's *Twelfth Night.*

Mordecai after punching Rigby in the arm. "Everybody knows that. Duh!"

"I can't keep track of everybody's nickname!" Rigby rubbed his arm where Mordecai had socked it. "Dude, you totally gave me a dead arm. Good job. But that means you have to carry the posters."

Mordecai sighed and adjusted the bundle in his arms. "Let's just go and get these posters up, dude. But first, let's go check out that abandoned campground." He looked toward a wooded part of the Park, where smoke, as if from a campfire, was rising. "Looks like Benson was right—somebody's camping over there."

"But, Mordecai—what if the campers are really witches? I don't want to get turned into a frog!"

"Witches? Dude—Benson was just trying to freak us out. It's probably just some hobos eating cans of franks and beans, and singing hobo songs around the campfire. Maybe if we get them to leave,

Benson will give us a day off or something."

"A day off? Let's go roust some squatters, then!" Rigby ran off in the direction of the fire.

"Witches," said Mordecai, shaking his head as he followed Rigby. "What does Benson think this is, *Macbeth*? Yeah, right."

CHAPTER 2

At the same time that Mordecai was shaking his head in disbelief, the three witches were sitting around a campfire in a clearing in the Park, having just finished their breakfast (Blandene made oatmeal). Behind each of them was a tent. Putricia was playing *Witch Wars*, Blandene was knitting, and Cronella was staring into an empty teacup, attempting to work a divination by reading the tea leaves at the bottom.

"Hmm," muttered Cronella to no one in particular. This was usually her cue to get someone to ask her what she saw.

"Do you see anything, dear sister?" asked Blandene, taking the bait.

"No, it just looks like tea to me," Cronella

responded grumpily. "Nothing new, though my witch senses tell me that we can expect visitors soon."

"Witch senses, Cronella?" asked Putricia, not looking up.

"Yes. My ears. The two fools approach and they're very loud."

Cronella was right. Beyond the edge of the clearing, two arguing voices could be heard, and they were getting closer.

"I'm telling you, dude, Taco'Clock has the best guacamole in town, hands down!"

"Better than the Avocado Dome? I don't think so."

"Well, how are we going to settle this, then?"

"There's only one way: a Guac-Off."

"Guac-Off!"

Mordecai and Rigby walked into the clearing, with Mordecai still cheering the idea of a guacamole-tasting war. Not paying any attention, they tripped right over the stake line of the witches' tents, falling to the ground.

"What the heck, man?!" Mordecai said, getting up and dusting himself off. "Who put this tent here?"

"Uh, Mordecai?" Rigby said, having noticed the three women sitting around the dying campfire, looking at them. "I think THEY did."

"Who's they?" Mordecai said as he turned around. Seeing the three women, he grinned awkwardly. "Oooooh-kay. This might seem like a strange question, and feel free to say no, but are you guys, like, witches?" said Mordecai.

"There are hobo witches squatting in the Park?" added Rigby helpfully.

"Shut up, dude," Mordecai warned Rigby through clenched teeth. "If they're W-I-T-C-H-E-S, they might not like being called H-O-B-O-S." Turning back to the three women, Mordecai continued, "Because if you ARE witches, and you ARE camping in the Park, our boss wants you to leave."

Cronella's eyes grew wide.

"Listen, buster," she said. "What if we ARE witches? AND we're hobos? What are you going to do about it? We've got magic spells for DAYS. Who wants to be a frog, huh? Who?!"

"Not me!" Mordecai said. "You know what they say—'Witches give stitches.'"

"It's true," said Blandene, clicking her knitting needles in an almost menacing way. "They DO say that. And we do. If you cross us."

Rigby ran over to where Putricia was sitting hunched over her game.

"Hey, are you playing *Witch Wars*?" Rigby said to Putricia as he peered over her shoulder.

"I sure am."

"Wow—you've made it to Level Sixty-Six! How did you get past the Frost Giants on Level Fifty-Seven?"

"You've got to save the fireball power-up you get on Level Forty-Nine. Don't use it before you run into the Frost Giants."

"Duh! Of course! Man, you're cool. For a witch."

"Thanks. You're cool, too. For a raccoon."

"If you two are finished flirting—"

"We're NOT flirting, Cronella!" protested Putricia as she put down her handheld game.

"We're just talking video games!" said Rigby, jumping away from Putricia (but not without glancing at her and cracking a smile).

"Well, if you are finished talking about video games, let's get down to business." And as Cronella began to speak, clouds gathered and darkened in the sky above, and thunder sounded in the distance. "You two knaves—"

"Who you calling *knaves*, witch lady?"

"Excuse me. Though seemingly mere pawns, you two FOOLS are key players in the events that are coming. To that end, attend well to our witchy words. Blandene: Puck's faery dust, please."

Blandene reached into her fanny pack and took out a jar, from which she poured some fine powder into her hand. Holding up her palm, she stood in front of Mordecai and Rigby, and blew the powder into their eyes.

"Augghh! That stings!" said Mordecai, rubbing his eyes.

"Ow! What gives, lady?" added Rigby, blinking away tears.

Blandene looked at the jar in her hand.

"Oh my, I'm SO sorry. That was salt," she said, shrugging. Throwing the jar to the side, she peered intently into her fanny pack and withdrew another jar, this time looking at its label closely. "Aha! This is what I was looking for!" Pouring another small amount of powder into her hand, she blew it again into their eyes, and this time, instead of cringing,

Rigby and Mordecai both instantly relaxed and smiled. Rigby began to drool a little bit, in fact.

"Good job, Blandene," said Cronella. "Now let's get these idiots on their merry way." With that, Cronella began to chant in her prophecy voice, "Go forth into the world, with posters fair to post."

Blandene added: "Place one over your rivals', whom it would anger the most."

And then Putricia took up the chant, "A thoughtless act of idiocy will increase the odds . . ."

Together, the three finished in eerie unison: "Of invoking an ancient theater curse by bringing forth the THEATER GODS."

Still under their spell and dripping drool all over, Mordecai and Rigby looked on slack-jawed as the witches raised their hands to the sky. Lightning bolts shot from their fingertips and sizzled as they were absorbed into the clouds, and the ground rumbled and quaked. And then, as suddenly as it started, it was over. Rigby and Mordecai shook their heads and looked around the clearing—they were the only people there. Looking up, the sky was blue and there wasn't a cloud in sight. Mordecai turned to Rigby.

"Dude, did you hear thunder?"

"Nope."

"For a second there, I had the weirdest feeling that . . . nah, you'll think I'm going crazy."

"C'mon, tell me!"

"Well, I totally felt that we met those witches that Benson was talking about and that they cast a spell on us or something."

"Oh man, you ARE going crazy!"

"Ugh, I knew I shouldn't have told you. Anyway, let's go get these posters up before Benson tracks us down." Mordecai began to walk away toward the Park's exit, but Rigby lingered for a moment and looked around the clearing. For some reason, he had the strangest desire to play *Witch Wars*. Not only that, he was SURE he knew how to beat the Frost Giants on Level Fifty-Seven. Shrugging, Rigby scampered after Mordecai.

"Hey, dude," he said. "Wait up! What about our Guac-Off?"

CHAPTER 3

Rigby had just stapled a poster for the Park's Shakespeare Festival to a telephone pole and was panting with exhaustion. He turned to Mordecai.

"Gah! I'm sick of putting these posters up. How many more do we have?"

Mordecai flipped through the posters he was holding.

"Well, Benson gave us forty-five posters, and that was definitely the first one we put up, sooooo . . . one down, forty-four to go."

"Aw man. We're never gonna get this done." Rigby folded his arms. "You know what? I think we've earned a break. What about you?"

Mordecai looked around, uncertain. "I dunno, man. Maybe we should get at least a few more up before we slack off . . ."

"Dude, don't be like that! It's kind of hot out here, don't you think?"

Mordecai looked up at the shining sun and wiped some sweat from his forehead. "It IS a little warm."

"And we're right around the corner from the Coffee Shop . . ."

Mordecai nodded. They WERE super close to the eatery their friend Eileen worked at. "True . . ."

"And they have fresh-squeezed lemonade . . ."

A vision appeared in Mordecai's mind of a dancing lemon wearing sunglasses while holding a frosty glass of ice-cold lemonade. "Also true . . ."

"AND I heard they have *Alley Brawlerz 5*, the latest *Alley Brawlerz* game."

Mordecai could almost hear the beautiful sound of the arcade machine's attract mode, a tough voice that growled, "Oh yeah? You wanna brawl with me?!"

followed by the even sweeter sound of a quarter dropping into the coin slot.

"*Alley Brawlerz 5*?! Sold. Let's go."

A few moments later, they were in front of the Coffee Shop, and they were about to walk through the door when something taped to the window caught Mordecai's attention—it was a poster advertising the East Pines Shakespeare Festival.

"Check it out, Rigby. Somebody from East Pines has been here already."

"Well, too bad for them, because we're here now. I've got an idea, dude. Gimme one of those posters."

Rigby pulled one of the posters from Mordecai's hands and carefully placed it over the East Pines poster, taping it up so that it covered the other one completely.

"Heh, heh, heh. Two posters down and forty-three to go. Now let's get some lemonade."

Rigby walked through the doors of the diner and

spotted Eileen working behind the counter, holding a pot of coffee. When Eileen saw them, she smiled.

"Mordecai! Rigby! Hi! Come sit at the counter," she said, waving them over. Mordecai and Rigby sauntered over and sat down.

"What are you guys doing here? Aren't you supposed to be at work?" she asked, leaning on the counter.

"We ARE working, Eileen, thank you very much," said Rigby. He pulled a poster from Mordecai's stack and showed it to her. "We're the advertising crew for the Park's Shakespeare Festival, and we're putting up posters all around town. Tough work, but you know us—we're real theater buffs."

Eileen snatched the poster from Rigby's hands and squealed. "Oh, I'm so excited! I LOVED last year's puppet show." She scanned the poster quickly. "The Merrie Players?! Are you kidding? This is going to be great! What's the secret show?"

"Well, actually—" began Mordecai.

"Wait, wait, don't tell me! I want it to be a surprise. Can I keep this one and put it on my wall? Pleeeease?"

"Yes! Another one bites the dust. Only forty-two to go," said Rigby.

"Awesome!" said Mordecai. "I didn't know you were such a big Shakespeare fan, Eileen."

"Are you kidding? Check out my button." Eileen pointed to a small circular pin attached to her uniform, which Mordecai and Rigby had to lean close in to check out. The middle of the button featured a skull with Shakespeare's haircut, and around the skull, spiky punk-rock letters spelled out the phrase SHAKESPEARE RULES, OKAY?

"Ooh. Cool button," said Mordecai.

"Thanks! I made it myself. I LOVE Shakespeare," Eileen said. "In fact, one of my dreams is to be in a Shakespearean play one day.

But I don't know if I'll ever get the chance." Eileen sighed and looked out the window wistfully. Mordecai and Rigby looked at each other.

"Um, can we order?" said Rigby.

Eileen shook her head to clear the cobwebs. "Oh, sure! Sorry. Just daydreaming about iambic pentameter, ha-ha! What'll it be?"

"Two ice-cold lemonades for two hard-working—"

Ding-ding! The bell on the front door of the diner rang, interrupting Rigby mid-order.

"Oh no," Eileen said. "Not these guys again."

"What guys?" Mordecai asked as he and Rigby swiveled around on their stools to see who had walked in. His stomach dropped when he saw three of the bootlicking employees from East Pines Park, their sworn archrivals. They stood in the doorway, sneering.

"Well, well, well—if it isn't Whatshisname and his little furry flunky from the Park, out promoting their cute little Shakespeare Festival," the lead one said, walking up to Mordecai and Rigby. He was holding a crumpled-up piece of paper in his hand and unfurled it so his buddies could see it.

"I found this outside over one of our posters. Oooooh—the Merrie Players!" he said sarcastically as he read the information on the poster. "And a SECRET play! Aren't WE scared?" He and his buddies laughed dismissively, and then he crumpled up the poster again and threw it into a nearby trash can.

"Forty-two posters to go, Mordecai!" Rigby whispered excitedly. "Ow! Stop hitting me!"

Mordecai jumped up and got into the lead flunky's face, fuming. "Why'd you do that, man? Go find somebody else's poster to crumple up. And it's not just a Shakespeare Festival, it's a SHAKES-PERIENCE."

"Oooh, a 'Shakes-perience.' Pardon *me*. That changes *everything*, doesn't it, guys? Haw, haw, haw."

"You're being sarcastic, right?" said Rigby.

"Duh! Of course I'm being sarcastic! You think

you guys have a shot to get the Gilded Globe this year after that puppet-show disaster last year? Fat chance! East Pines rules the Shakespeare Festival circuit in this town. Get used to it, and get ready to lose again this year. Losers." As he finished, the lead East Pines flunky fixed Mordecai with a glare and, bringing his hand to his mouth, bit his thumb.

The other two flunkies and Eileen all said, "Oooooooooh."

Mordecai and Rigby looked at the East Pines guys like they were crazy, which seemed like the most likely explanation for what was going on.

"Um, dude—are you biting your thumb at me?" said Rigby. The lead flunky nodded, thumb still being bitten.

"Excellent Shakes-burn," said the second flunky.

"Good reference, man," said the third flunky. "Well timed, too."

"That's . . . really weird," Rigby said.

"It *is* weird, Rigby, but biting your thumb at someone was a mortal insult back in Shakespeare's time," said Eileen. "Haven't you ever seen *Romeo and Juliet*?"

"Seen who?" Rigby said.

"*Romeo and Juliet*! Shakespeare's most famous play. Really?"

Rigby's face was blank. He shook his head. "Nope, never heard of it. Doesn't ring a bell. Are you sure that's the title?"

Eileen folded her arms on the counter, put her head down, and sighed heavily.

"Okay, so you're biting your thumb at us," said Mordecai. "Now what? Do we bite ours or something?"

The lead flunky took his thumb from his mouth. "Now what? Normally after a good thumb-biting, we'd brawl in the streets. But Gene's forbidden brawling until after the festivals, so we have to settle this insult some other way. Hmm. Let me see . . ."

The lead East Pines flunky and his two flunky friends huddled in a circle and began to discuss their plan, occasionally looking up to make sure that Mordecai and Rigby didn't try to sneak out on them. Mordecai and Rigby shrugged and began to sip on the lemonades that Eileen had just handed them.

"What are you guys going to do?" Eileen asked, whispering.

"I have a plan," said Mordecai. "Check it out."

Putting down his drink, Mordecai took a straw from the dispenser on the counter and tore off its end. Putting the exposed end in his mouth, he aimed the straw at the lead flunky and blew, sending the straw wrapper directly into his ear and causing him to bat at his head, thoroughly annoyed.

"Hey! What gives?" said the lead flunky, breaking the circle. He and his fellow flunkies came chest-to-chest with Mordecai and Rigby.

"I'll tell you what gives," said Mordecai. "Gene

doesn't want you guys brawling in the streets, and Benson doesn't want us to, either. But that doesn't mean we can't brawl . . . in the *Alley*!"

Mordecai pointed to the *Alley Brawlerz 5* machine that was tucked into the corner of the diner, and almost on cue, its attract mode began. The thumping electro-rock of the *Alley Brawlerz* theme began and a voice rumbled from the game: "Oh yeah? You wanna brawl with me?!?!"

A sly look came over the face of the lead flunky, and he smiled.

"Let me get this straight: You're challenging me to a DUEL? An *Alley Brawlerz* duel?"

"Uh-huh." Mordecai nodded. "The loser has to buy the winner's lunch. And has to put up the winner's posters all over town."

"Interesting stakes," said the lead flunky as he rolled up his sleeves. "I accept your challenge. But I have to warn you—we've had every *Alley Brawlerz* game at the East Pines snack bar since they've been making 'em, and I've had the high score FOREVER."

"Whoop. Dee. Do," said Mordecai grimly. He and the lead flunky walked over to the *Alley Brawlerz 5* machine, followed by Rigby and the other two flunkies. Standing before the cabinet, they were bathed in the flashing lights that emanated from the screen; the *Alley Brawlerz 5* logo appeared and then broke apart, torn asunder by a disembodied fist, which then proceeded to pound the letters into dust to the beat that pumped from the machine's speakers, and for a moment the warring factions of the Park and East Pines were united in awe of what had to be the most excellent video game on earth at that moment in time.

"Whoa," said Mordecai reverentially. "It's so beautiful."

"Wow," agreed Rigby. "Is it weird that I want to kiss it?"

Mordecai and the East Pines flunkies all shook their heads no. Snapping out of his trance, Mordecai produced two quarters and placed them in the groove right above the joysticks at the bottom of the screen.

"Following the ancient rites and traditions of arcade challenges, since I challenged you, I'll put up the quarters for the game," Mordecai said.

"Following the ancient rites and traditions of arcade challenges, I shall take the quarters and put them in the machine," said the East Pines flunky. He dropped the first quarter in the machine, and a voice boomed from the speakers: "Press Start, Player One!" As he dropped the next quarter in, the voice said, "Right on! A challenger! Press Start, Player Two!"

Mordecai's and the lead flunky's fingers hovered over their respective Start buttons.

"On three," said Mordecai. "Count it off. One . . ."

"Two," said the lead flunky.

"Three!" they said at the same time, and pressed their buttons simultaneously, and the ground underneath the diner shook, moved by the mega-bass rumbling from the machine.

"Choose. Your. Brawler!" commanded the machine's voice as a selection screen came up, offering them the choice of twenty-four different brawlers. Mordecai moved his joystick to select Fauntleroy Smack, a gentleman brawler from the nineteenth century. The East Pines flunky chose Cyrille Chaos, a Mohawked punk from the future. After their selections, the machine rumbled again.

"Choose. Your. Weapon!" A selection of deadly implements appeared on the screen, and Mordecai, being Player One, was given the decision. He moved the cursor over a box at the bottom-right corner of the display: a set of deadly-looking rapiers.

"You know: swords because of Shakespeare," he said, shrugging. The flunky nodded. There was only one more option to select.

"Choose. Your. Alley!" A new screen appeared, this one showing alleys from throughout time and space, each one with its own ins and outs. There was a Roman alley, a modern city alley, a space colony alley, and more, but this time it was Player Two's turn to make the selection, and the East Pines flunky bypassed all those cool alleys and moved the cursor over the one right in the middle of the screen: an alley in Renaissance Italy.

"If we're going to riff on *Romeo and Juliet*, we might as well take it all the way, right?" said the lead flunky. Mordecai nodded.

"I don't get it," said Rigby. "What does Italy have to do with *Romeo and Juliet*?"

"Shut up, Rigby," said Mordecai. "We're about to DO THIS."

The lead flunky pressed the button to confirm the choice of alley, and when he did, the machine shot out a beam of light from the screen, causing everybody around to squint. "All right, everybody, gather 'round," said the machine. "It's time for a BRAWL!!!"

The light faded, and there, on the screen, stood Fauntleroy Smack and Cyrille Chaos, both wielding long rapiers. The East Pines flunky acted first, jumping up and arcing toward Fauntleroy, sword aimed directly at his heart. Mordecai reacted quickly, pressing buttons to first parry the strike and then moving the joystick to tumble backward and into a ready position. For a moment, the two fighters stood there, moving up and down in an animation cycle, staring each other down. But then, there was a flurry of activity as both Mordecai and the flunky began to furiously mash buttons. Their fighters leaped, rolled, and flipped back and forth, stabbing and slashing at each other as Renaissance Italian spectators cheered them on on-screen.

It turned out that the East Pines flunky wasn't kidding: He was seriously skilled, and with his mastery, Cyrille Chaos took the upper hand, climbing up on a balcony overlooking the alley and coming down on Fauntleroy's head with the handle of his rapier, knocking him out cold. Round one was over, and East Pines was victorious. The two other flunkies cheered loudly for their leader while Mordecai fumed. Rigby poked him.

"You can't lose, Mordecai! I can barely put up our posters, much less THEIRS."

"Chill, dude. There are two more rounds to go," Mordecai said.

"We'll see about that," said the lead flunky. "All I've got to do is beat you again and you'll be out there putting up our posters in the hot sun while we kick back in here and have lunch and lemonades."

"Your lemons aren't squeezed yet," said Mordecai, and the second round began. At first,

Cyrille Chaos had the upper hand. The East Pines flunky relentlessly attacked Fauntleroy Smack with wild slashes that were slowly wearing away at his health. But Mordecai was thinking, and the flunky was overconfident. Biding his time, Mordecai waited until he was sure that his opponent was going to rely on brute-strength attacks, and that's when he deftly guided Fauntleroy to tuck into a ball and roll through Cyrille's legs, winding up behind him, refreshed and ready to fight. Discombobulated, the East Pines flunky struggled to regain his advantage, but it was too late. The tables had turned! After a brief exchange of parries and thrusts, Fauntleroy swiftly delivered the final strike directly to Cyrille's heart, winning the round.

"Yes! Dude!" yelled Rigby, ignoring the grumbling coming from the East Pines crew.

"Yeah, I sometimes like to let my opponents win the second round to give 'em a sense of false hope," said the lead flunky with a smirk. "Looks like it worked."

Mordecai cracked his knuckles and set his jaw. "That sounds like something someone who's afraid he's gonna lose would say."

"Why, you little . . . !" began the East Pines flunky, who looked as if he was ready to fight Mordecai right there in the diner, but he was interrupted by the machine.

"Last brawl, winner takes all!" barked the machine. The third and final match had begun, and this time, something was . . . different.

Tendrils of colored smoke began to issue forth from the bottom and back of the machine, wrapping the interior of the diner in a rainbow fog. The lights from the screen were brighter, illuminating the faces of the players with an eerie luminescence and hypnotizing the spectators, causing everybody to have a particularly strange shared hallucination:

On the screen, Fauntleroy Smack and Cyrille Chaos had somehow morphed into Mordecai and the East Pines flunky. And this time, the battle in the alley was being fiercely fought by both sides from the beginning, with neither Mordecai nor the flunky giving any quarter. If Mordecai slashed, the flunky parried. If the flunky stabbed, Mordecai sidestepped. It was an epic, furious duel! They leaped onto carts as their swords flashed. They grabbed conveniently placed bars and did somersaults off them. They ran up and down staircases, their blades clanging and ringing.

It felt so real and so crazy that Rigby and the other flunkies felt the need to actually duck when Mordecai and the flunky ducked. It might have been the greatest fighting game match ever played, in fact, all the way up until the end!

Both characters were bloodied and dangerously low on health when Mordecai managed to actually execute one of the most difficult *Alley Brawlerz* moves in the book: the Double Disarm, which caused the flunky's sword to fly out of his hand and into Mordecai's. Knowing his defeat was imminent, the flunky's character kneeled down to yield, and Mordecai placed his swords on either side of his neck. There was a pause, and then . . . *snicker-snack*! Mordecai cut his opponent's head clean off.

"This brawl is OVER!!!" cried the machine. "Fauntleroy Smack is the BOSS BRAWLER!" And with that, a light shot out from the screen, bathing the interior of the diner in blinding white illumination. And then, as quickly as it started, the light went out and everything was back to normal, sort of. The smoke had cleared. The game was over, and Mordecai had won. But the East Pines flunkies were more than furious, for not only had they lost, but the energy that shot out from the screen had somehow burned their uniforms away, leaving them clothed only in their hats, undershirts, boxers, socks, and shoes. They looked, in a word, ridiculous.

"Heh, heh," Mordecai said, offering his hand for the lead East Pines flunky to shake. "Good game?"

The flunkies' faces were all changing to various ugly shades of red and purple, as if they were emotional surfers hanging ten on a tasty wave of embarrassment and rage.

"Screw Gene's rules! You two and us are going to rumble RIGHT NOW!"

"Here!" cried Mordecai as he picked up his roll of posters and threw them at the lead flunky. "Make sure you get 'em up all over town!"

"Charge these jerks for our lemonades, Eileen!" yelled Rigby as he and Mordecai burst through the diner's doors.

"Get 'em, guys!" yelled the lead flunky, and he and his crew followed Mordecai and Rigby through the doors, hot on their tails.

Mordecai and Rigby raced down the sidewalk, weaving in and out of the way of pedestrians who looked at them as if they were crazy, which, to be fair, wasn't unfair, for they both had wild looks on their faces.

"Those guys are pretty mad about the whole duel thing, huh?"

"Talk about sore losers!" said Mordecai.

"They're gaining on us! What are we gonna do?"

"There!" Mordecai pointed to the intersection they were approaching. The DON'T WALK sign was blinking . . . and then it stopped.

"We've got a couple of seconds before the light changes. If we can get across, maybe they'll get stuck and we'll lose 'em."

"Let's go!"

Mordecai and Rigby poured on the gas and ran out into the road, but it was too late. They didn't have the light anymore, and they found themselves right in the sights of oncoming traffic! Cars swerved around them as they dodged in and out of their way. A horn began to blare, and Mordecai and Rigby turned to see a huge vehicle bearing down on them, tires squealing. Faced with what looked like inevitable death-by-pancaking, they did the only thing they could think of doing—they screamed like little babies.

"Aaaaaaaaahhhhhh!!!"

CHAPTER 4

The piercing screech of brakes filled the air as a gigantic tour bus came to an abrupt halt in front of a cowering Mordecai and Rigby, barely stopping in time and with only inches to spare. The vehicle, which looked to have been a school bus in a previous life, was decorated in jaunty colors and was pulling a trailer, and on both sides, painted in multicolored Olde English letters, were the words THE WORLDE-FAMOUS MERRIE PLAYERS.

"Dude," Rigby said, still shaking in fear. "Do you think this is the Merrie Players' bus?"

Mordecai smacked his forehead and sighed, then walked over to the door on the bus's side. The door opened with a *whoosh*, and sitting at the steering wheel was a silver-haired man dressed in a full-on

Renaissance Faire getup, complete with tights.

"Well met, squires," the man said. "Mayhap you could direct myself and my humble band of thespians to Ye Olde Parke? For we are the Merrie Players, and we have come to put on a show!"

A lusty cheer of "Huzzah!" came from the back of the bus. The driver nodded sagely in agreement.

"*Huzzah* indeed, my friends." The driver turned to Mordecai. "My name is Galahad, Galahad Thrillington. And who might YOU be?"

"My name's Mordecai, and this is Rigby. We actually work at the Park," Mordecai said.

"Then fortune smiles upon us Merrie Players! Clamber upon our trusty convcyance and direct us to yon Parke, sirrahs!" Even though he had actually said *Park*, Galahad had one of those awesomely fake, sort-of-British accents where he rolled his *r*s and you could tell that he was adding *e*s to the end of words, at least in his mind, and he was such a good actor that you could hear the invisible *e*s, too.

"Uh, what?" Rigby said.

"Just get on the bus and give us directions, guy," said Galahad in a normal but exasperated voice. "We've been on the road all day and could really use some showers and some shut-eye before we do some rehearsing."

"A shower! A shower! My kingdom for a shower!" someone shouted from the back.

"All RIGHT already, Felix! You'll get your shower! Like none of us have ever heard a King Richard III joke like that ever before. Jeez," Galahad said crankily, nodding toward the back of the bus. "You see what I'm dealing with here?" he said to Mordecai, who nodded. Galahad glanced into his rearview mirror, and a look of concern troubled his eyes. "Hey, check out this gang of park ranger guys coming up the road. They're dressed in their underwear, and they look pretty mad. Are they friends of yours?"

Mordecai and Rigby looked behind the bus and saw the East Pines crew running toward them, shouting.

"Nope!" said Mordecai, dragging Rigby off the ground and onto the bus. "Definitely not friends of ours. Let's go! Take your first left at the stoplight. And, you know, floor it."

Galahad grabbed the lever for the door and pulled it closed in the faces of Gene and the guys from East Pines, who banged on the side of the bus with their fists, getting further enraged as Mordecai and Rigby made faces at them through the glass. Galahad pressed the gas pedal to the floor, and the bus skidded around the corner, leaving the East Pines crew behind in a cloud of dust and exhaust.

CHAPTER 5

Before long, the Merrie Players' bus pulled through the gates of the Park(e), and Mordecai guided Galahad to a small, seldom-used campground, a spot where they could park the bus, set up camp (in addition to being famously skilled, the Merrie Players were known for their practice of pitching and living out of beautiful tents near wherever they were performing), and use the nearby facilities. Galahad parked the bus, killed the engine, and opened the front door. The rest of the Merrie Players—a motley assortment of men and women—piled off the bus and into the campground, doing cartwheels and calisthenics, and set up camp. Galahad, accompanied by Mordecai and Rigby, got off last, and when Galahad stepped onto the ground, he kneeled and kissed the dirt.

“I give thanks to the Theater Gods that we, the Merrie Players, have arrived safely once again to bring Shakespeare to the people!” Galahad said, still on his knees. “To this, I cry huzzah!”

“Huzzah!” echoed the rest of the Merrie Players. Galahad looked at Mordecai and Rigby, and arched his eyebrow expectantly.

“Huzzah?” they said at the same time.

“Excellent! We’ll make thespians of you two yet. Help me up, my knees . . .”

“But what play are we doing?” asked Mordecai.

“Oh, but I cannot say its name,” said Galahad.

“Why not?” inquired Rigby.

“Because of . . . the *curse*!” Galahad looked even more serious than he already seemed. “If you were to speak the name of the play in the theater, you would doomed.”

“That’s silly. There’s no such thing as curses, just tell us the name!” demanded Rigby.

"Yeah, man, just tell us!" insisted Mordecai, even louder.

"Say it! Say it! Say it! Say it!" they both began to chant in unison, getting louder and louder, until finally . . .

"*MACBETH*!" said Galahad. "We're doing *Macbeth*! You got me to say it. Are you happy?!"

A chilly wind began to blow, softly at first, but quickly developing into a gale, causing people to grab anything handy to avoid being swept away. Thunder sounded, and rain began to fall in a downpour.

"Oh no! You idiots have really done it now!" shouted Galahad over the sound of the storm.

"What's happening?!" Mordecai said.

"You got me to say the name of the Scottish play out loud before the performance, and the Theater Gods must have been listening. They're onto us!"

"That doesn't sound so bad. What's a Theater God, anyway?"

"Doesn't sound so bad? Look around you!"

And as he said those words, a crack opened in the ground, directly under the Merrie Players' bus. For a moment it teetered on the edge, but the crack widened, and the bus tipped . . . and fell into the chasm with a crash!

"Our bus!" Galahad said. "I just painted that!"

The crack in the ground got even bigger, and flames from the wrecked bus shot up. From the depths, two huge hands emerged, grabbing the edges of the hole and pulling up an equally huge body, at least twenty feet tall, dressed like a comic-book version of a Shakespearean actor, complete with tights and a doublet. And atop its shoulders were two heads that wore plain masks. One mask was smiling and the other was frowning—the traditional comedy and tragedy masks of drama. The giant figure stepped out of the hole and stared down at Mordecai, Rigby, and the Merrie Players, who cowered beneath their gaze.

"The Theater Gods," choked Galahad. "We are SO boned."

As the wind continued to whip around them, a sad voice came from beneath the tragedy mask. "Galahad Thrillington of the Merrie Players, you have broken one of the cardinal rules of the fellowship of the theater."

"I know, but these guys MADE ME do it. It was them!" said Galahad, pointing wildly at Mordecai and Rigby. "Oh Theater Gods—have mercy on us!"

Rigby turned to Mordecai and said, "This is really messed up, dude."

"Oh, you think?!" Mordecai said sarcastically.

The giant clapped its hands together, and crackling energy began to jump between its hands and its eyes. There was a pause as it let the energy gather, and then suddenly it extended its arms, and the energy shot out from its two hands and four eyes, twisting and turning around and striking the Merrie Players even as they ducked for cover. In an instant, all the Merrie Players, from Galahad down to the understudies, were turned into stone statues, all of them in mid-dramatic poses.

The Theater Gods' dual gazes turned to Mordecai and Rigby, and the comedy head spoke in a jaunty tone.

"All right, fellas. It's up to you. If you want to help these jerks out and break the curse, you need to make an offering to us. It's gotta be something spectacular, so get a gang together and put on a show. If we dig it, then *boom*, no more curse. If not, you've got a new sculpture garden on your hands."

Straddling the hole in the ground, the Theater Gods jumped up . . . and fell into the depths below, disappearing from sight. A moment later, its hands reached up and pulled the hole closed. And as quickly as it began, the wind stopped.

"Huh, a lot of weird weather lately, don't you think?" said Rigby.

"Who cares about the weather? Oh man, Rigby. This is bad. This is really bad. What are we gonna DO?!"

"I've got it!" said Rigby.

"What?"

"Who do we know who regularly deals with crazy supernatural stuff like this?"

If this were a cartoon, lightbulbs would have appeared over Mordecai and Rigby's heads. They both snapped their fingers.

"Skips!" they said at the same time, and ignoring the jinx for expediency's sake, they ran off to find their wise yeti friend. If anybody could figure a way out of this mess, it'd be him.

They hoped.

CHAPTER 6

Soon, Mordecai and Rigby were standing in front of the Park's temporary theater, which, as advertised, looked just like a classic drama pit of Elizabethan London.

"Wow, Skips wasn't kidding. This place is awesome. I hope we keep it after the festival," marveled Rigby.

"No time for architecture appreciation, dude. Skips has gotta be in here somewhere." Mordecai ran through the theater's doors and into its interior, which was open to the sky, just like a vintage theater. There, on the stage, sat Skips in the lotus position, meditating. He liked to relax like this every time he finished a big project. Mordecai and Rigby jumped on the stage, pacing back and forth and waving their arms maniacally.

"Skips! We need your help!" Rigby shouted.

"Yeah, man. We made some weird gods really angry and they turned the Merrie Players into statues and now we don't have a play!" added Mordecai.

Skips opened one eye slowly and regarded his idiot coworkers.

"We really did it this time, Skips! Benson's gonna kill us," said Rigby.

"The Shakespeare Festival is coming up soon and the Merrie Players are out of commission and we don't have a play. Benson's definitely going to fire us and then kill us!" said Mordecai.

"Actually, I disagree. I think he's going to kill us, THEN he's going to fire us!"

"Whatever, Rigby! Either way, we're DOOMED!"

"Are you guys finished?" asked Skips, opening his other eye while still remaining in the lotus position.

Mordecai and Rigby stopped pacing and began conferring among themselves.

"Weird and scary Theater Gods . . ."

"Check."

"Merrie Players turned to stone . . ."

"Check."

"Shakespeare Festival ruined . . ."

"Shakes-perience. Check. Yeah, that's about it," Mordecai said.

Skips rubbed his chin thoughtfully, uncrossed his legs, and stood up. "Good, because I think I've got an idea."

"Really?" Mordecai asked. "What is it?"

"First off, we've gotta call a meeting. Get everybody over here. Everybody EXCEPT Benson."

"And then what?" Rigby asked. Skips turned to him and narrowed his eyes.

"Then? Then we need to talk to Death."

CHAPTER 7

Before long, all of the Park's employees (except for Benson) had gathered on the stage of the theater. Muscle Man, Hi-Five Ghost, Pops, Thomas, Mordecai, and Rigby all looked at Skips.

"Okay, then. Let's get started. I bet you all are wondering why I called you here. Well, you can thank Mordecai and Rigby. Long story short, they invoked an ancient theater curse and got the Merrie Players turned into magic statues by a two-headed freak that calls itself the Theater Gods. And no Merrie Players equals no Shakespeare Festival."

"What?! No Merrie Players? Dudes! You ruined it!" Muscle Man screamed and ripped off his shirt and threw it at Mordecai and Rigby, who recoiled from both his anger and the smell of his clothes.

"Tut-tut," said Pops, shaking his head in disappointment. "Bad show, fellows. Bad show." Thomas and Hi-Five Ghost also shook their heads.

"Okay, okay," said Mordecai. "We get it. We really messed up this time."

"'This time,'" said Hi-Five Ghost while making air quotes with his ghostly head hand.

"Good one, Fives! Up high!" said Muscle Man as he slapped Hi-Five Ghost's hand.

"We've already assigned the blame," said Skips, "but now we've gotta work together to fix this. If not for Mordecai and Rigby's sake, at least for Benson's."

"Can't we just, like, hire another traveling theater company?" asked Rigby. "If you've seen one, you've seen 'em all."

Skips shook his head. "No can do. The Merrie Players are the BEST. Without them, we've got no hope of winning the Shakespeare Festival battle, and guess what happens after that. That's right:

You're *fired*. So basically, this situation is impossible, and to salvage it, we've got to do the impossible. And to do *that*, we need to bring in some heavy hitters, starting with . . . *Death*."

"Aw, not THAT guy," said Rigby. "He's such a jerk."

"Quiet, dude," said Mordecai, looking around shiftily. "He might be listening. Death is everywhere."

"Are you guys still on speaking terms with him? 'Cause we're going to need his help if my plan is going to work."

"Uh, sure, I think so. Heh, heh." Mordecai laughed nervously and scratched his head.

"Whattaya mean, 'I think so'?" Skips asked.

"C'mon, man—he's Death. He's not really on good terms with *anybody*, if you know what I mean," Mordecai replied, pulling a finger across his throat.

"Yeah, he's kind of a cranky guy," Rigby agreed, "especially if you're babysitting his kid. Why do we need to bring Death into this, anyway?"

"We need him because we have to talk to an old roommate of mine. He might be uniquely qualified to help fix this colossal screw-up."

"Great! What's his name and number? Let's just call him up," said Mordecai as he took out a cell phone.

Skips shook his head.

"You can put that away. We can't reach him using conventional methods. This old roommate of mine has been dead for four hundred years."

Skips turned to Mordecai and Rigby.

"Back when we were roommates, I used to call him *Wild Bill* because he was such a crazy guy, but you guys might know him by his other name . . ."

Skips paused for dramatic effect.

"WILLIAM SHAKESPEARE."

Rigby's eyes got big.

"And if we're going to contact Shakespeare in the afterlife, we're going to need the help of somebody who's got easy access to the netherworld. That means we need Death's help, so you guys better work on your groveling. Let's go."

Death sat on his couch in his living room, long hair unfurled, mustache waxed, dressed in his typical outfit of boots, jeans, T-shirt, and vest, one leg crossed over the other, his arms spread, as Mordecai, Rigby, and Skips pleaded their case before him. So far, he seemed unimpressed.

"So you need me, the Grim Reaper, the personification of Death itself, to go fetch a soul from the afterlife so you can take it on a field trip? I dunno, mates. Some things just can't be done. I'm afraid I'm going to have to say no. It'd set a bad precedent, you know what I mean?"

"See, Skips?" Rigby whispered. "He's kind of a jerk."

"Oi! I heard that!" said Death testily.

Mordecai looked at Skips and whispered, "Shoot, now what are we gonna do about the Theater Gods?"

"The Theater Gods!" said Death. "Why didn't you say that in the first place?! Those weirdos have been driving me crazy for millennia. And those two creepy faces? Brrrrr. I'd do anything to put a kink in their curtain, you know what I mean?"

Death got up from the couch and began pacing, index fingers on his skull-y temples, thinking hard.

"So it's Shakespeare you want, eh? One of my favorite writers. Lots of killer death scenes in his work. Fantastic stuff. Okay, let me see, where in the afterlife IS he? Hmmm . . ."

"Whattaya mean, *where*?" asked Skips.

Death stopped pacing and turned to the fellas. "Imagine the biggest suburb in the world and multiply that by a million and *that's* the afterlife. Billions of souls all living in weird developments with names like 'Maplewood Terrace,' 'Greenbriar Place,'

'Greenwood Heights'—it's like a massive cemetery crossed with a massive subdivision. Boring place, the afterlife. Aha! THAT'S where he is."

Death snapped his fingers, and a spectral rotary phone that looked to be made of various bones appeared, floating before him. Picking up the receiver and putting it to his ear, Death dialed a number and waited. And waited. And waited some more. He looked at the guys.

"A lot of dead people don't have voice mail," he said, shrugging. "They're weird like that. Ah! Somebody's picking up. Oi there! Is this the funereal home of Shakespeare? Yeah, it is? Mr. WILLIAM Shakespeare? The one and only? Fantastic, fantastic. What do you mean, *Prithee, who is calling?* You don't recognize my voice? It's only the personification of DEATH, mate. Anyway, get ready to get summoned. I've got some people here who want to speak to you. Okay? Okay. Hanging up now . . . Bye . . .

No, you hang up first . . ."

Death hung up the phone, which disappeared in a puff of brimstone. "One playwright's ghost, coming right up!" Death snapped his fingers, and a circle of fire leaped up from the floor, forcing Skips, Mordecai, and Rigby to recoil. But as soon as it started, it died down, and between them and Death stood a man. A man with a mustache and a pointy beard, dressed in strange, antiquated clothes, who would have looked like any player from your local Renaissance Faire had he not been (a) floating a few inches above the ground and (b) transparent. He looked around Death's living room, and when he saw Skips, he broke out in a wide grin.

"Skips! My old friend! The Falstaff to my Prince Hal, the jelly to my peanut butter. Good to see you! Once more unto the breach, eh?" Shakespeare moved over to give Skips a hug, but his arms passed through Skips's body. "Whoops! Forgot about being a spirit there for a second. My bad."

"*My bad*? That doesn't sound like the Wild Bill I used to know," said Skips.

"I'm a playwright, Skips! As language evolves, so do I. New phrases and elocutions are my meat and bread. And I also live next door to a dead surfer. He's rad." Shakespeare turned to look at Mordecai and Rigby. "And who are these good gentlemen you travel with?"

"Guys, meet my old roommate: William 'Wild Bill' Shakespeare. Wild Bill, meet my friends Mordecai and Rigby. We need a favor from you."

"Hail, fellows. Well met," said Shakespeare, raising his hand in greeting. "Any friend of Skips is like unto the same to me. I'd shake your hands, but, well, you can see I have a slight corporeal deficiency. What can I do you for?"

"Wait—*Wild Bill*?" said Rigby. "I thought he was *the Bard*. He has ANOTHER nickname? Ow!

Stop giving me dead arms, Mordecai!"

"This is the greatest playwright in the English language EVER, Rigby. Show some respect," said Mordecai. "Anyway, Mr. Shakespeare, here's the deal . . ."

Shakespeare's ghost listened intently as Mordecai, Rigby, and Skips told him about the events of the past day, starting with Benson's dream of winning the Gilded Globe and ending with the invocation of the theater curse. When they had finished their story, Shakespeare nodded sagely.

"Unlike most tales told by idiots, this one has sound and fury AND signifies something. A *Shakes-perience*? I like the sound of it, and I'd like to help save it. But to truly help you, I must go back to the land of the living, and to pass from Death's realm into the world of mortals, I must have a vessel. Who would do me the honor of being my host? As Skips can attest, I am a decent roommate. Ah! Thank you, Rigby!"

"What?! I didn't . . . hey!"

Rigby looked to his left and to his right and saw that both Mordecai and Skips were pointing at him. He knew he had no choice.

"Okay, fine," said Rigby. "Get the possession over with already, okay?"

Shakespeare's ghost floated over to where Rigby stood, moving into the same space as Rigby and causing Rigby to shudder uncontrollably, as if he were freezing.

"S-s-s-so c-c-c-cold," Rigby said through chattering teeth.

"That's just the icy hand of death brushing against your soul, my friend," said Shakespeare. "It'll be over anon. Here we go!"

The outline of Shakespeare's ghost grew bright for a moment, then drew into itself until it was a bright ball of energy in the middle of Rigby's chest. Rigby began to twitch wildly, moving his body like a break-dancer with a sugar rush and shaking his head back and forth. And then . . . he stopped, eyes wide, totally still. The ball of light faded into his chest and he opened his mouth and said:

"BURRRRRRRRRPPPPPPP!"

And then he passed out, crumpling to a heap on the floor. Skips and Mordecai kneeled down beside him.

"Oh, man," moaned Mordecai. "Rigby's DEAD!"

" 'E's not dead," said Death. "I should know: I'm an expert. He's just got possession sickness. Give him—or them, I guess—a few minutes, and they'll be all right."

Death looked at his watch.

"Ah, the wife should be home any minute now. Time for you guys to get out of my house! Give those Theater Gods a kick in the rear for me, eh?"

Death snapped his fingers again, and his three houseguests disappeared in a puff of brimstone and lightning and a thunderous explosion.

CHAPTER 8

Crack-a-boom!

Mordecai, Skips, and the possessed Rigby fell from a hole in the sky to the ground, directly in the middle of the abandoned campground where, unfortunately, the Merrie Players remained stone statues. Skips and Mordecai sat up, dazed, but Rigby was still out cold, and he wouldn't wake up, no matter how much they shook him.

"Wild Bill? Shakespeare? Rigby? Are any of you in there?" Skips asked as he kneeled over Rigby.

"What's going on, Skips? Why isn't he waking up?" Mordecai asked.

"I don't know. Maybe it was the shock of getting possessed by a ghost? There's all sorts of supernatural stuff going on that even I don't understand."

But at that moment, as if he had been jolted by a thousand volts of energy, Rigby jumped up, wide-eyed and bushy-tailed, and looked back and forth, surveying his surroundings in wonder.

"Zounds! 'Tis awesomely true! I have shuffled back into the mortal coil and am once again rude flesh and blood. This rules!"

"Shakespeare!" said Skips.

"Rigby!" said Mordecai.

"Nay. I am neither, yet I am both. A chimera of flesh and spirits! If thou hast to name me, name me . . . SHAKESBY!" said Shakespeare, er, Rigby, er, Shakesby, with a flourish. Skips and Mordecai gazed at their new/old friend in awe, and Shakesby looked down at his body in shock. "Alas! I am without a stitch, and that is a most alarming sitch. Crave your pardon."

Shakesby looked around and spotted the trailer that had been attached to the Merrie Players' bus.

Opening the trailer's door, Shakesby jumped in, and for a moment the trailer rocked back and forth. It sounded like Shakesby was rummaging through trunks and such, looking for something. "Aha!" came a cry from the interior, and Shakesby jumped out of the door, dressed in tights, leather boots, a flowing white shirt, and an embroidered vest. He looked exactly like what you'd picture a playwright from early-seventeenth-century England would look like, actually.

"Now to business we must attend. Skips, my old roommate, how do ye fare?" Shakesby said.

"I'm good, Wild Bill. It's nice to kinda see you," replied Skips.

"Aye, 'tis good to see you as well."

Mordecai got close to Shakesby and peered at him intently. "I don't get it," he said. "Are you Shakespeare or are you Rigby?"

"Both, friend Mordecai. Ha-ha! I am a confus'd

soul, an alchemical mixture of the radness of both Shakespeare and Rigby. The best of both worlds and the worst of none, I daresay. Shall we party? I have such a craving for soda."

"Later, Wild Bill. We'll party later. Right now, we need your help," said Skips.

"Aye, I know," said Shakesby, tapping his head with his forefinger. "You guys are, as is the saying now, 'totally screwed,' are you not? Your players are idle, and you are without a play."

"That's about the long and short of it," said Skips. "The Merrie Players were going to put the Shakespeare Festival—"

"The Shakes-*perience*," interrupted Mordecai.

"Pardon me, the Merrie Players were going to put the Park's SHAKES-PERIENCE over the top, and without them we don't have a chance. At least we didn't until we brought you back from the afterlife. With you, we can cook up something really special, and we need it. Our boss really has his heart set on winning this contest."

"I've been wondering about that," said Mordecai. "Why IS Benson so bent out of shape over this? I mean, it's only a dumb theater trophy."

Skips looked surprised. "You mean you don't know what happened to Benson back in high school? About the play he was stage-managing?"

A very Rigby-esque conspiratorial look came across Shakesby's face, and he pulled a notebook from a vest pocket. From another pocket, he took a quill and ink. Sitting down, he opened the book, dipped the quill, and waited for Skips to continue.

"Ooh, the plot thickens. Do tell, for I, Shakesby, am always on the lookout for good material."

At that moment, Benson drove up in the Park's golf cart. Riding with him were Muscle Man, Pops, Hi-Five Ghost, and Thomas. The cart came skidding to a halt, and Benson jumped out, followed by everybody else. Naturally, he looked like he was on the verge of an epic freak-out.

"We tried to distract him, dudes!" said Muscle Man, but Benson pushed him aside and looked around in disbelief at his singed workers.

"What. The. Heck. What was that NOISE? It sounded like someone lit a match in a fireworks store. And what the heck are YOU doing here, Mordecai and Rigby? You're supposed to be out hanging posters! And look, Thomas—it's the Merrie Players' trailer, but where are the Merrie Players? And what's with these statues? And why are you dressed like that, Rigby?!" Benson threw his clipboard to the ground in a fury as his face contorted in rage. "Can somebody tell me what the heck is going on here?!" he fumed.

"Benson, old man!" said Shakesby. "You know me, yet you do not. I am your vassal Rigby, but once again I am another, the writer known as Shakespeare, and I am at your service. Mordecai and Rigby helped to bring down an ancient curse 'pon yon Players, and my old roommate Skips called me forth from the undiscovered country to aid you in staging your show. I am Shakesby, and I am at your service." As he finished, Shakesby bowed low in front of Benson.

Benson stared at Mordecai, Skips, and Shakesby, who were looking at him, smiling expectantly.

"You three have lost your minds," he said with certainty.

"Look around you, Benson. It's true: The Merrie Players have been cursed," said Skips. "If we don't do something, the Shakes-perience is over, and you'll lose the Gilded Globe to East Pines again."

Benson was examining one of the statues intently as Skips talked. "This statue looks EXACTLY like Galahad Thrillington, the leader of the Merrie Players," he said.

"Benson, it looks like Galahad Thrillington

because it IS Galahad Thrillington," Mordecai said.

Benson put his hand to his forehead. "So, what you're saying to me is that the Merrie Players are CURSED, and you two"—he pointed at Mordecai and Rigby—"are responsible?"

There was a pause as Skips, Mordecai, and Shakesby all looked at each other, then turned back to Benson.

"Pretty much," said Mordecai.

Benson nodded calmly. "Okay. I get it now. It's over. No Merrie Players, no Shakes-perience, no Gilded Globe, no nothing. All my planning was for nothing because I trusted you two with putting up some posters. Of course! Well, what's done is done."

Benson began to walk back to the cart, but as he did, he raised a finger, as if to indicate he'd forgotten something.

"Oh, I forgot one last thing," Benson said as he turned around. "Mordecai and Rigby? You're FIRED!"

CHAPTER 9

"C'mon, Benson, be reasonable. You can't fire them now. People are coming to the Park and expecting a Shakespearean play. We need their help. Shakesby is the only one who can save the show now," said Skips, putting his hand on Benson's shoulder to calm him.

"I suppose you're right, for the moment," said Benson. "But after this is over, they're DEFINITELY fired."

"Okay, it's agreed, we'll do a different play. What were you thinking, Shakesby?" said Mordecai. "Got any ideas?"

"I need to sit down," said Benson.

"And inspiration is what I doth crave," said Shakesby.

"Whattaya mean, *inspiration*?" said Skips. "Let's just stage one of your old plays."

"In the speech of the times, I have been there and I have done that. In my salad days, when I was alive, I used to use anything I could get my hands on to provide inspiration for my plays. I'd lift plots and characters from everywhere. And I feel I must do the same now."

"But we don't have TIME for that, Shakespeare. I mean Rigby. I mean Shakesby," said Mordecai.

"We have the time, and I have an idea. Patience, fellows! I know from whence to gain creative footing, and I shall be back anon! Talk amongst yourselves!"

And with that, Shakesby ran off, leaving his friends to stare at his backside.

Hours later, Shakesby calmly strolled back into the abandoned campground to the surprise of his friends and coworkers, who had been combing the neighborhood and the surrounding area trying to find him. He was munching contentedly on a box of movie popcorn.

"Wild Bill!" said Skips. "Where'd you take off to? We looked all over town for you."

"As I foretold, I have been seeking inspiration, and I daresay I've found it," said Shakesby.

"Dude, where did you find it?" asked Mordecai.

"Yeah, I can't wait to hear where this is going," Benson added.

"My dear fellows, I attended a marathon showing of *Occult Cop* at a place in town you call a movie theater. Very lovely space, I might add. Who would have thought seats could be so comfortable?" Shakesby paced back and forth, deep in thought and exclaimed, "I shall write, with haste, a buddy-cop action play."

"Dude, but you're not just gonna steal someone else's ideas?" inquired Mordecai.

"I have always stolen plots and inspiration from lives, loves, and deaths other than my own," Shakesby replied with a nod of his head. "And so I must begin." And he walked away.

CHAPTER 10

"But, Benson, you HAVE to be the stage manager. NOBODY'S bossier and meaner than you!"

"Thanks, gu—wait, what?!"

Skips stepped between Benson and the guys just as Benson began to turn an awful shade of red. "What Mordecai and Rigby mean to say is that you know how to run things. This Park would've fallen apart years ago if it weren't for you. Right, everybody?"

Everybody nodded in agreement. Benson might have been a hard, demanding boss, but they knew what Skips said was true.

"Okay," Benson said.

"No problemo," said Larry the Laser Wizard

as he pulled a thick collection of sheet music from the secret compartment in his piano bench. He was sitting in his garage/rehearsal space, surrounded by keyboards. Around his feet, dry-ice smoke curled, and the garage was lit by pulsing lights. "I just so happen to have a score I wrote a while back for a canceled Laser-Rama show at the Planetarium based on *Moby-Dick*. After that, I tried to use it in a production of *The Legend of Robin Hood on Skates* at the local roller rink, but that went south. Been itching to use it for something, and this sounds like the perfect project. What's it pay?"

"Uh, nothing," said Rigby.

Larry the Laser Wizard frowned.

"But I think we're getting catering from Taco'Clock," said Mordecai.

"Taco'Clock?! Why didn't you say so? They have the best guacamole in town!"

Larry the Laser Wizard stood up and drew

himself to his full height of five feet and six inches.

"Hand me my cape, guys—you've got yourself a Laser Wizard for your play." As Rigby grabbed Larry's green-and-purple cape from the peg it was hanging on, Larry opened up the door from the garage to the house. "Mom! I'm going out!" he yelled. "I got a date with Shakespeare!"

"Should I put your dinner in the oven, honey?" called a voice from inside.

"Yes, please!" Larry yelled back. Closing the door, he fastened the cape around his neck. "Let's go make theatrical history, shall we?"

⁂

The entire cast and crew of *MacDeath and Juliet* had assembled in the temporary theater, and Shakesby took the stage to address them.

"Thomas, my factotum, please pass out the scripts."

Thomas walked among the crew and the cast,

handing each of them a small booklet. Mordecai held his up.

"Uh, Shakesby—this looks great and all, but the premiere of the Shakes-perience is supposed to be TOMORROW," said Mordecai. "How are we going to learn our lines and rehearse the play in one day?"

"When one has been dead for four centuries, one picks up a trick or two," said Shakesby, moving his hands in an odd way. The books in everybody's hands began to glow, a glow that slowly spread up their arms, down their bodies, and around their heads until each member of the company was bathed in golden light. Shakesby snapped his fingers, and as suddenly as the glow began, it was gone. Its effects lingered, though, for everybody standing in the pit looked at each other in wonder.

"Dude," said Mordecai, dumbfounded, "I know this play."

Everybody nodded, because *they* knew the play,

too. Backward and forward, front to back, they had it memorized.

"You wrote this, Rigby?" asked Eileen, impressed.

"Yes. No. Kind of," said Shakesby. "Shakespeare, who I am, wrote it, but Rigby, who I also am, is part of it. His love of B-grade cop action movies is what inspired the creation of the play, and his extensive knowledge of the tropes of said genre was invaluable when it came to actually putting pen to paper."

CHAPTER 11

Benson was standing in the wings of the stage, looking particularly frantic. Skips approached slowly.

"Benson, man, you look terrible," said Skips.

"I'm beyond stressed. What if everything falls apart? What if everything goes wrong? What if . . . ?" he said, unable to finish his sentence.

"Everything is going to be fine. You'll see," Skips tried to reassure him.

"But you don't understand. I can't fail again, not like that . . . ," Benson cried.

"Benson, what are you talking about?" Skips inquired patiently.

"It was a long, long time ago, back in my senior year of high school . . ."

Benson looked around the backstage area and let out a contented sigh. There was nothing he liked better than to be the calm center of the panicked hubbub before an opening night, and this one was going to be a performance to remember. High school was about to end and he was stage-managing his last production as a senior.

"Benson, you got the dry ice ready for the curtain?"

"Locked and loaded, P-Nice."

"Did anybody see my cape? Where's my CAPE?!"

"Your cape is hanging up on the back of the door of your dressing room, Marvin."

"How's the crowd, Benson?"

"We've got a full house, Abby."

"Benson! Benson! I can't remember my lines!"

Benson put down his trusty clipboard and put his hands on his colleague's shoulders. He looked him square in the eye.

"You know your lines," he said. "You may not know that you know them, but you know them, you know what I mean? They're not in here." Benson pointed to his friend's head. "They're in here." Benson pointed at his friend's heart. "Now get out there and deliver the best performance that you can. I'll be back here stage-managing everything and looking out for everybody. We're not a family, we're a high-school theater company."

Benson's friend's eyes grew big and watery. "That's the most inspirational speech I've ever heard, man."

"Thanks, but YOU inspire ME. Now go out there and break a leg."

And that's exactly what happened. Benson fell off the stage as soon as he got onto it, breaking his leg and ruining the play.

⁂

"Don't worry, Benson. Everything will be fine!

Now get out there and introduce the play!" said Skips as he pushed Benson out of the wings and onto the stage. At first, Benson blinked at the assembled crowd—it was huge, or at least it seemed huge from where he was standing. Looking around, he saw eager faces staring at him from the pit, theatergoers hoping to see something neat. He glanced up at the box and balcony seats and scanned the faces there. They were mostly normal folks, but on one end he saw three ladies sitting together who kind of looked like witches. In the middle box, there was someone who looked as if he had two heads, one covered in a tragedy theater mask and the other in a comedy theater mask. On the other end, he saw a long-haired metalhead who seemed to have a skull for a face. *Theater enthusiasts sure are weird*, Benson thought as he shook off his stage fright and walked to the middle of the stage. It was so quiet, you could hear a cricket dropping a pin.

"Welcome, everybody, to the Park's fifth annual Shakespeare Festival. This year, we have a surprise for you."

"WE WANT THE MERRIE PLAYERS!" cried a voice in the audience.

The crowd roared its approval and began to chant, "MER-RIE PLAY-ERS! MER-RIE PLAY-ERS! MER-RIE PLAY-ERS!"

This was getting ugly. Benson started to sweat and looked over to stage right, where his crew was standing in the wings. They all smiled nervously and gave him a thumbs-up.

"Um, I'm afraid that the Merrie Players won't be performing tonight," Benson said to the crowd, who began to boo. "They're, uh, indisposed."

"I want a refund!" came a shout.

"LET'S RIOT LIKE THEY USED TO IN GOODE OLDE ENGLAND!" yelled some idiot. The audience roared even louder, and a few of the surlier theatergoers began to try to climb onstage. Fortunately, Muscle Man and Hi-Five Ghost saw these interlopers before they could pull themselves up and quickly knocked them back into the crowd with their batons.

"Shut up and listen to what the man's trying to say, people!" said Muscle Man. "He's trying to usher in a bold new era of theater." As he said this last line, he brandished his baton threateningly. Everybody in the crowd stopped talking.

"Thank you, Muscle Man. Yes, it's true, the Merrie Players WON'T be performing tonight, and for that I apologize. But instead, we've got something even better: a new, never-performed play by WILLIAM SHAKESPEARE."

The crowd started murmuring among themselves immediately, and the tone was half disbelieving, half excited.

"A new play by Shakespeare? Impossible!"

scoffed one theatergoer.

"Omigodthisisamazing!" somebody else screamed.

An old man climbed onto the shoulders of the heavy-metal dude standing next to him and leveled an accusing finger at the stage. "Frauds! Bamboozlers! Scam artists! This isn't Shakespeare, it's FAKESPEARE! Fakespeare in the Park, I say!"

Inspired by this pun, the crowd began chanting again. "FAKESPEARE IN THE PARK! FAKESPEARE IN THE PARK! FAKESPEARE IN THE PARK!"

Benson held up his arms for quiet, and after a few moments, the crowd subsided, although the old man who began the chant kept trying to get them going again. "I assure you that what you are about to see is one hundred percent REAL," said Benson, "but it's Shakespeare like you've never experienced him before. Now, without much more ado—ha-ha, get it? *Much ado*?—I present to you . . .

"William 'Wild Bill' Shakespeare's *The Most Awesome Exploits of MacDeath, a Veteran Constable, and Juliet, His Squire*! Or, Shakesby's *MacDeath and Juliet*. It's kind of a complicated story, but anyway. You can sit back, relax, and absorb the spectacle of the play, but if you're confused, please pass around the complimentary commemorative scripts we've placed in stacks around the theater. They're there to help you follow the action, and believe me, there's plenty of that.

"And by the way, one last bit of warning: There are a lot of flashing lights, so if you have a medical condition, you might want to watch out. And to everybody standing within fifteen feet of the stage, you're in the splash zone, so watch out during the third act. It's fake blood, but still, there's a lot of it, so . . ."

The crowd began to murmur excitedly as Benson ran off the stage. Looking around, Benson saw his crew staring at him expectantly. Fixing his mouth into a determined scowl and picking up his trusty clipboard, Benson slipped his headphone radio on and spoke into the microphone. "Let's do this thing, guys. Cue the lights. Pops, you're on."

The lights dimmed, and the orchestra, led by Larry the Laser Wizard, began playing the overture. Pops, dressed in silver tights, a red shirt with a lightning bolt on it, a gold cape draped over his shoulders, and a wizard hat on his head, stepped out onto the stage and into the spotlight. The audience held their breath. The play had finally begun.

THE MOST AWESOME EXPLOITS OF MACDEATH, A VETERAN CONSTABLE, AND JULIET, HIS SQUIRE

Dramatis Personae

Chorus

(played by Pops)

Caleb, a patrol constable

(played by Muscle Man)

Felix, another patrol constable

(played by Hi-Five Ghost)

MacDeath, a veteran constable

(played by Mordecai)

Juliet, his young squire and new partner

(played by Eileen)

The Chief, the chief constable

(played by Gene)

Skull Wizard Prime, a villain

(played by ???)

Skull Wizard #1

(played by Skips)

Skull Wizard #2

(played by Thomas)

The Mayor

(played by Shakesby)

ACT I

SCENE I. A SEEDY-LOOKING CITYSCAPE

[Enter CHORUS.]

CHORUS:

Two parks, similar in sylvan glory,
The insult from prank wars never to mend,
Are the players in this theater story,
Crosstown archrivals to the bitter end.
In the hazy time of summer's fierce heat,
When fancies doth turn to things of the beach,
A new fight begins, but not in the street,
But 'pon the stage, and in poetic speech.
Featuring ghosts, explosions, rock and roll,
Sword fights, wizards, and a laser-light show.
'Tis a crazy tale, with only one goal:
To make one shout a hearty cry of "Ohhhhh!"
A cooler play you've not seen, we would bet,
Than this one of MacDeath and Juliet.

[Exit Chorus. Enter Caleb, a young patrol constable, carrying a lantern.]

Caleb:

The streets are quiet, like unto a tomb, but even a grave has sounds of grief or merriment. Nay, the streets are quiet and quiet again by too great a measure.

[Enter Felix, another young patrol constable, carrying a lantern, walking backward. Neither Caleb nor Felix sees the other, and they collide, falling into a heap while fighting.]

Felix:

Halt, villain! For I am a constable. This is my beat, and beat you I shall, for that is my sacred duty.

Caleb:

Hold, dear Felix. It is I, Caleb, fellow constable. We have met in the break room at the station, and over coffee and donuts matters of the day discuss'd.

Felix:

Caleb, fair esteemed colleague. I crave your pardon. Look about—hast thou noticed things peculiar?

Caleb:

The silence, you mean?

Felix:

The very same. 'Tis strange, is it not? Portents and forebodings of an ill sort overcome me. My instincts thus raised, investigate I shall.

Caleb:

And where does your eye wander?

Felix:

To the decrepit building yonder.

Caleb:

Hold, good Felix. For backup we shall call, for without support we should fall.

Felix:

True words you speak, friend Caleb. But who can aid us in our hour of need?

[Enter MacDeath, a cop, with his new partner, Juliet, a rookie.]

MacDeath:

Tarry not, Juliet. Mine stool pigeon hath sung, and the tune he calls is sweet to mine ears: The lair of the Skull Wizards is nearby. They hatch fiendish plots and noisome schemes, unawares of our presence.

Juliet:

The Skull Wizards, my captain?

MacDeath:

Indeed. For years they hath been my sworn enemies, and now yours.

Caleb:

MacDeath! A legend by any other name would be as badass.

Felix:

Great cop and seeker of corruption! Then the rumors are not true and you have not retired to a life of leisure on your boat, to fish for the rest of your natural days afloat?

MacDeath:

Retirement is nigh, dear Felix, and this be my last case. Fear not, for soon fish, and not criminals, shall face my wrath. Attend to my words:

[MacDeath delivers a soliloquy on his career and past cases before entering the Wizards' lair.]

MacDeath:

Halt, villains, for justice is upon you.

Skull Wizard #1:

Alack! MacDeath has found us, and we are foiled. Our evil plots forever spoiled.

Skull Wizard #2:

Cruel twist of fate! Take this, MacDeath, a violent epistle, violent projectile: magic missile!

Skull Wizards #1 & #2:

Magic missile, magic missile!

[JULIET pushes MACDEATH to the ground, and the SKULL WIZARDS' bolts instead strike the wall, which explodes. The set begins to shake.]

Skull Wizard #1:

Our aim untrue, MacDeath lives, yet mischief has still been wrought. Feel now the very timbers shake. The walls tumble, and my escape I make!

[Exit SKULL WIZARD #1 in a cloud of smoke and fire. Debris falls from the ceiling, and dust gathers in clouds.]

Skull Wizard #2:

Abandoned by friend and hunted by foe, I must not tarry. News to our superior I must carry. I bid you the Spaniard's Farewell to a Child.

MacDeath:

Hasta la vista, baby!

[Exit Skull Wizard #2 in a cloud of smoke and fire. More debris falls from the ceiling, and even more dust gathers in clouds.]

ACT I

SCENE II. THE CHIEF'S OFFICE

[Enter the CHIEF, who paces back and forth, agitated.]

Chief:

The events of the afternoon trouble my mind. I, Chief of Police, have heard reports of mayhem afoot in our streets, and at the root, one of my own. Enter, friend MacDeath, attended by your squire.

[Enter MACDEATH and JULIET.]

MacDeath:

Good morrow, Chief. Wherefore are we summoned? Unlikely though it is for a detective such as I, I have not a single clue. I pray thee, elaborate.

Chief:

Dost thou wonder why I seek an audience? I am most wrathful! Rogue cop that you are, you have made mockery of our office. Witness these scrolls heap'd upon my desk like shovelfuls of dung.

MacDeath:

Sonnets of love, no doubt.

Chief:

Merrily you jest, but nay, they are not love notes meant to woo, or notes of affection sent to you. These are warrants from our Mayor that demand thy head.

MacDeath:

Do you mean to give them satisfaction?

Chief:

Thinketh me such a craven, my son? I stand between thee and doom, and shall always. But a price must be paid.

MacDeath:

What cost then?

Chief:

Exile. You are hereby released from my service, MacDeath. Thy badge of office and thy sword, that ye have named Skullbane, shall stay here upon my desk.

MacDeath:

A plague on the house of the Mayor! So be it. If the Skull Wizards shall this town burn, then I shall watch the flames from a distance, on a peaceful sojourn.

Juliet:

If exile is MacDeath's fate, then let it also be mine.

MacDeath:

Hold, rash Juliet. I give you one last order: remain and be steadfast. Forswear not your city and fellow cops.

Juliet:

Very well. I shall stay.

Chief:

You are the best of us, MacDeath.

MacDeath:

This, above all things, rings true. I take my leave and salute both of you.

[Exit MacDeath.]

ACT II

SCENE I. THE *VIOLA*, MACDEATH'S BOAT

[Enter JULIET, carrying a six-pack of soda.]

Juliet:

Ho there, crew of the *Viola*. Permission to come aboard?

MacDeath:

How now, Juliet? Permission granted, if thou carries a six-pack of soda.

Juliet:

My fare is paid, then.

[JULIET boards the *Viola* and opens sodas for herself and MACDEATH. They toast.]

MacDeath:

Do you bring news of the city, friend Juliet?

Juliet:

Aye, I do. In the fortnight since your retirement, the Skull Wizards run rampant in the streets. The police force, thus overwhelmed, is routed.

MacDeath:

Retirement chafes upon me, as if it were an undergarment a size too small! Would that the Chief could restore me to my rank and return my sword, Skullbane, to my hand.

Juliet:

It sits behind his desk in a place of honor.

MacDeath:

As well it should, Juliet.

[MacDeath looks up and sniffs the air.]

MacDeath:

Hark! Dost thou hear that? Upon the wind, a faint whistling.

Juliet:

Look there, a projectile, incoming! Leap, MacDeath!

MacDeath and Juliet:

Ahhhhh!

[MacDeath and Juliet jump from the deck of the *Viola* as a flaming missle hits the boat. The *Viola* explodes. Enter the Skull Wizard Prime, floating above the stage.]

Skull Wizard Prime:

I am the Skull Wizard Prime! I shall gather the Skull Wizards at our temple and revel in this outcome. Ha-ha-ha-ha!

[Exit the Skull Wizard Prime. MacDeath and Juliet climb onto the dock.]

MacDeath:

They think us dead, Juliet, and that shall be their undoing. My keen mind is afire, a plan therein brewing.

Juliet:

How now, MacDeath?

MacDeath:

Make haste to the office of the Chief, and once there, seek ye the both of you an audience with the Mayor. I shall see thee anon.

Juliet:

Dost thou have a plan?

MacDeath:

Thou know'st it, my friend.

ACT II

SCENE II. THE TEMPLE OF THE SKULL WIZARDS

[A good number of SKULL WIZARDS are gathered. Enter SKULL WIZARDS #1 AND #2.]

Skull Wizard #1:

Have you heard the news? MacDeath is slain.

Skull Wizard #2:

The rumors then are true. By whose hand?

Skull Wizard #1:

The Skull Wizard Prime.

Skull Wizard #2:

Truly he is the master of disaster.

[Enter SKULL WIZARD #3.]

Skull Wizard #1:

Halt, stranger. You are unfamiliar to us.

Skull Wizard #2:

Present thy evil credentials.

Skull Wizard #3:

I am, er, Larry, of the Skull Wizards from the East Side of Town. Perhaps thou hast heard of me, my evil deeds thus renowned?

Skull Wizard #1:

The name of Larry strikes fear into my heart. Hail, fellow evildoer. Well met.

Skull Wizard #2:

Our master approaches. Bow low.

[Enter the SKULL WIZARD PRIME from above. The SKULL WIZARDS all bow.]

Skull Wizard Prime:

With my powers fantastic, I float 'pon the air;

look upon my skull head, cower, and despair! Unawares I caught MacDeath, and through means magical I have blown his boat sky-high. With our foe out of the way, our victory, thus assured, is nigh!

Skull Wizard #1:

Three cheers for the Skull Wizard Prime!

Skull Wizards:

Evil, huzzah! Evil, huzzah! Evil, huzzah!

Skull Wizard Prime:

And now, though I seek not to offend, off we must be, one more evil matter to attend.

[Exit the SKULL WIZARD PRIME and SKULL WIZARDS #1 AND #2.]

[SKULL WIZARD #3 turns to the audience and pulls back the cowl of his robe, revealing the face of MACDEATH.]

MacDeath [aside to audience]:

My disguise, undiscovered, has confirmed my darkest suspicion. Now I must fly to the Chief's office, there to finish my secret mission.

[Exit MacDeath.]

ACT III

SCENE I. THE STATION HOUSE

[The Chief paces in his office. Before him sits the Mayor, and behind the Mayor stand his two bodyguards.]

Mayor:

I grow impatient, Chief Constable. For what was I summoned?

Chief:

'Tis a mystery, though Juliet, a most noble constable, assures me of its import. Here comes she now.

[Enter Juliet.]

Chief:

Juliet! The Mayor, made to wait, is most vex'd. Speak and explain thyself.

Juliet:

I have not the words, my Chief, but perhaps our friend can.

[Enter MacDeath.]

Chief:

MacDeath! What means this?

Mayor:

MacDeath lives, though rumors of his death abound!

MacDeath:

Your forgiveness I crave, Chief, for my subterfuge. Mayor! Stand accused of treachery!

Chief:

Has retirement caused thee to take leave of thy senses? Is this charge serious?

MacDeath:

As an attack of the heart. Witness his deception!

[MacDeath jumps the Mayor. They tussle, and MacDeath pulls the Mayor's skin from his head, revealing the face of the Skull Wizard Prime.]

MacDeath:

The Mayor is none other than the head of the serpent, the Skull Wizard Prime!

[The Chief grabs MacDeath's sword from behind his desk, throws it to MacDeath, and draws his own sword. He and MacDeath hold the Skull Wizard Prime at sword point.]

Chief:

Freeze, deceiver! Thou art under arrest.

Skull Wizard Prime:

Unmask'd am I, and all the better to perform my wicked deeds free and unfettered. Nay, Chief. I shall not freeze. The chill of death is upon THEE!

[The Skull Wizard Prime zaps the Chief with magic electric death energy. The Chief falls.]

Chief:

I am slain! Avenge me, MacDeath!

Skull Wizard Prime:

I challenge thee, MacDeath! Let me be the sickness that shall forever still your breath.

MacDeath:

I would dance with thee, Skull Wizard Prime, to the tune of metal 'pon metal, which is sweet to mine ears.

Skull Wizard Prime:

Metal!

[A laser-light show begins, accompanied by a driving synthesizer and drum machine score, as MacDeath and the Skull Wizard Prime fight. Juliet fights the two bodyguards, who are revealed to be Skull Wizards #1 and #2. An explosion goes off.]

MacDeath:

A worthy foe, thou art!

Skull Wizard Prime:

Kneel before me, MacDeath. Your sword is not mightier than my magic!

[Battle, etc., continues. Juliet slays Skull Wizard #1. Another explosion goes off.]

Skull Wizard #1:

Argh!

[Battle, etc., continues. Juliet slays Skull Wizard #2. The Skull Wizard Prime blasts MacDeath's sword from his hand. Yet another explosion goes off.]

Skull Wizard Prime:

Now I shout a diabolical hooray: MacDeath hath fallen. Evil wins the day!

MacDeath:

Alack! I am bested.

Juliet:

Not while I stand at your side.

MacDeath:

Take up my arms, brave Juliet!

[MacDeath gives Juliet his sword.]

Skull Wizard Prime:

Brave novice, what hope have you to prevail, when your mentor, thus tested, did falter and fail?

Juliet:

There is wisdom in the philosopher's words: Let not your voice incur a debt that your rear end cannot settle one hundred percent!

[Juliet beheads the Skull Wizard Prime, and blood sprays from his neck, covering all the players.]

Skull Wizard Prime's Head:

Zounds!

Juliet:

Gross!

MacDeath:

If you pluck off its head, it doth bleed indeed!

[The Skull Wizard Prime collapses, neck still spraying blood. His body explodes. The laser-light show, etc., ends.]

MacDeath:

Our case hath ended. The Skull Wizard Prime, pierc'd by our swords, is no more. Juliet, with your able assistance, the Skull Wizard Prime has been destroyed, his butt presented hath been thoroughly kick'd. Now your aid I must employ to exit this place. My wounds are painful, yet not grievous, and my bones creak from all my years previous. Explosions have left the station in tatters, and speak I plainly—I am too age'd for these matters.

[Exit MacDeath and Juliet.]

END

CHAPTER 12

As the last line in *MacDeath and Juliet* was spoken, the curtains closed and the theater was quiet—TOO quiet. True to Benson's word, everybody within twenty feet of the stage was covered in stage gore, their clothes stained red permanently, probably. And then, in the silence, someone began to clap. Slowly at first, then gaining speed. Soon, other hands began to applaud, and then more, and then EVERYONE was clapping. It sounded like thunder, and the audience jumped to their feet and began to cheer loudly.

"Author, author!" shouted somebody.

"Woo-hoo!" yelled another.

"More MacDeath next summer!"

"Encore! Encore!"

"Forget an encore, how about a sequel?" screamed

the old man who had started the cry of "Fakespeare in the Park" before. Scrambling onto the back of the person in front of him, the old man jumped up onto the waiting hands of the crowd, began to crowd surf, and started a new chant: "Fakespeare rocks! Fakespeare rocks! Fakespeare rocks!"

The situation had degraded into complete and utter pandemonium, and it was AWESOME.

Backstage, the cast and crew gathered together in a circle as the hue and cry continued beyond the curtains. Everyone was pumped, excited not only that they had made it through the entire play but that it had been such a spectacular success.

"Holy moly," exclaimed Mordecai as he used a towel to clean stage blood from his face. "That was INCREDIBLE! Did you see how the audience ducked when the explosion went off at the end of the second act?"

"Verily did I witness their cowering, dude,"

said Shakesby with a chortle. "Oh, what fools these mortals be to be 'mazed by stagecraft. Three cheers for Muscle Man, who is like unto a sorcerer when it comes to special effects!"

"Woo-hoo!" said Muscle Man. "You know who else likes special effects? My mom! Really, she does. Especially the stop-motion animation of Ray Harryhausen."

"Quiet, everybody. Quiet!" said Skips. "That crowd is going to tear this place apart if we don't open the curtains soon and take a bow, but I think we should send someone out there first, someone to take the first bow."

Everybody nodded in agreement, and they all turned to look at one person standing in the circle, someone who was grinning as maniacally as the rest of them. Realizing that everyone was staring at him, Benson blinked slowly, looking somewhat stunned and taken aback.

"Me?" he said. "I don't know about that. How about Rigby? I mean Shakespeare. I mean Shakesby. He *wrote* the play, after all. Or how about the cast? You guys were INCREDIBLE. Especially you, Skips. And Eileen, your Juliet was tough *and* vulnerable. You guys deserve the credit, not me. I just stage-managed the play."

" 'Just stage-managed'?" said Mordecai. "Dude, without you, this whole thing would have been a disaster." Benson glared at Mordecai, who laughed nervously. "Heh, heh, I mean even *more* of a disaster. Your love of the theater brought us all together and made this possible. And it also saved a bunch of people from certain doom, so there's that. You were right: This WAS the best Shakespeare Festival ever. I mean Shakes-perience."

Everybody nodded solemnly in agreement, and Benson bowed his head.

"Thank you, everybody," he said. "I've been

waiting since high school to redeem myself, and you guys helped make it possible. Especially you two idiots." He nodded toward Mordecai and Shakesby, who smiled back at him.

"Anytime, Benson," said Mordecai.

"Aye, I second that. Anytime!" said Shakesby.

"But please don't make it a habit or EVER do this again," said Benson, who approached the spot where the curtains came together. "How about this? How about we all go out together? Thomas, pull the curtains!"

And at Benson's command, the curtains parted. The audience roared in delight, and the entire cast and crew of *The Most Awesome Exploits of MacDeath, a Veteran Constable, and Juliet, His Squire* took a long and well-deserved bow.

Later on, everyone in the production had assembled for the premiere after-party at the House.

Larry the Laser Wizard led a band in electro-rock versions of popular Elizabethan songs, and the dance floor was packed with revelers. Everybody was getting down, including the Merrie Players, who had transformed back into actors after the play concluded and who seemed downright cheerful considering they had just been stone statues. Benson, cup of punch in hand, watched his friends, coworkers, and rivals party together with a satisfied smile on his face.

"All's well that ends well," he said contentedly. Even those two idiots Mordecai and Rigby couldn't ruin it. In fact, they had inadvertently made it even better, not that he'd ever admit it to them. But then Benson noticed something: Everybody was partying in the living room except for one of those idiots—Rigby. Or Shakesby. Grabbing an extra cup of punch, Benson went in search of the World's Best Playwright/Worst Employee to congratulate him on a job well done.

— THE END —